The Bridge

GHODSI HOSSEINI

Tellwell Talent
www.tellwell.ca

ISBN
978-0-2288-3196-9 (Paperback)
978-0-2288-3197-6 (eBook)

I dedicate my story to my lovely family:
Afsin, Farzin, Daryoush and little Charli.

TABLE OF CONTENTS

FOREWORD

I am Ghodsi Hosseini, a woman from the land of beauty and ugliness, of originality and tradition, of justice and discrimination. Like tens of millions of other Iranians, I grew up in a religious family, and like millions of Iranian children I witnessed the revolution, war, corruption and ideological breakup of my country. Like thousands of Iranian girls with identities vastly different from our traditional mothers, I secretly fell in love, enjoyed my youth and connected myself to the outside world. Like a few women in my country, I chose my own husband. When it became too difficult for me and my family to struggle for freedom and the least human rights, we had to seek refuge in a safe country to raise our son in a new land and build a bright future for him far from war, destruction and the poisonous educational system.

This is my story about my first days of asylum in Germany and then my unintended trip to Canada, which happened for the sake of bad news. There I began to understand death, life and the beauty and ugliness of the world. I finally realized there is only one nation in the world called "humans" and only one country called "the world."

Ghodsi Hosseini

CHAPTER 1

Crossing

When she stood in front of the iron gate, she had made her decision. She knocked with her fist on the mouth of the gate. It was cold and stiff. Nana knew instinctively that something had to happen. The door opened its leady eyes and asked: "what do you want?"

Nana replied: "Crossing!"

The gate asked: "What do you know about crossing?"

Nana thought for a while. Sometimes you get just bored, frustrated or disappointed. You have to go. Why? You don't know. To where? You don't know. You feel like you have to pass and this feeling like a disease eats your nights and days. The passive state of nothing. Sometimes you think crossing means a beginning, change or rescue. Whatever it is, from a lost yesterday to an ambiguous tomorrow, makes no difference. So, absolutely the answer is the 'Crossing' itself. She felt pain in her heart for all that confusion, and tears rolled down from her eyes. The gate understood it was truly the time for Nana's crossing. It coldly and disappointedly opened its mouth and swallowed Nana, as well as her husband and son who were with her. Being swallowed was not a strange feeling. It was like diving into a swimming pool — a feeling of dizziness, loss and suspension. That feeling was like being captured and entranced by two eyes that only after hunting, in the hunter's dark belly, you realize you were hunted. Taste of death.

After passing the iron gate, there was a long, broad bridge in front of them. The first snowflake that landed on the Nana's hand melted, and its unique geometric shape was deformed and turned to a clear water drop. It reflected like a mirror the world around. Her journey on the bridge began. What could be waiting at the end of the bridge?

CHAPTER 2

Charlie

Nana and her family had not yet walked a few steps on the bridge when out of the fog suddenly a young, nude woman with black and tousled hair, a slim body and pale skin threw herself off the bridge while shouting: "Asyl, Asyl!"

Nana was scared and slowly asked: "What is Asyl!"

A voice behind her answered: "It means 'refugee.'"

Nana turned back and saw a little white dog that looked like a toy. He was waging his bobtail, trying to attract Nana's attention with his brown button-like eyes.

Nana asked: "Who are you?"

The poodle replied: "Charlie!"

"Where is your owner?"

"She was swallowed."

Nana rolled her eyes in surprise and asked: "What?"

Charlie answered sadly: "I don't know exactly. A friend of mine told me once, that to one of the bridge rules, I am not able to see her anymore you know what? There are some restricted rules here on the bridge."

"Oh, poor dog! What are you going to do now?"

"I'll take refugee in you!" And with his innocent eyes, he looked deep into Nana's eyes. Nana whispered while staring at the distance: "Refuge. The most beautiful and the ugliest experience in the world. The most beautiful when you take the refugee in the beloved's arms after so many years of being apart. The most beautiful when a child gets shelter in the mother's chest from fear, hunger and the strange world. The most beautiful when you are running from a heavy rain to a blue umbrella.

On the other hand, 'refugee' also can be the ugliest word, when you are landless or rootless and condemned to the humiliation of change in a land which belongs to others with their different laws.

Charlie didn't understand anything but still was waging his bobtail hopefully. His round brown eyes among curly hair on his lovely and slightly stupid face did their job.

Nana hugged him and made an excuse: "You can be a good friend to my son, little Dara, can't you?"

Charlie had lots of butterflies in his heart but he didn't say a word about not liking little boys or that he was afraid of them.

CHAPTER 3

Rules of the Bridge

What seemed like a black snake at the beginning of the journey, later was more like a big moving conveyor on which everyone and everything were moving at a very slow and intangible speed. People, trees, houses, parks and even rivers. There was no stoppage. Nana and her companions stood stunned while they were looking around.

Charlie told Nana: "Moving is the most important rule of the bridge; you have to move. If you don't follow this important rule, the next rule will come to you."

Nana asked: "And what is it?"

Charlie, in spite of his funny face, tried to look serious and after smelling a bush so carefully, he 'marked' it and said: "It's better first that I explain the second rule and then I will tell you the last one."

Nana looked at him with interest and said gratefully: "Okay! Let's hear them!"

Charlie carefully marked a tree that was near the bush, wagged his bobtail and said: "The rule of invisible strings! An intangible and undefined guidance that has many variants like the invisible strings of emotions, destiny, physics, metaphysics ... which are the source of too many stories that happen over days and nights, by moving over the bridge which has been called 'life.'" Charlie looked at Nana with a shame and said: "My friend told them to me but I don't know what exactly they are. And the last rule: staying motionless is equal to being swallowed by the dark and shadowy fog, which is like a devil doppelganger always following every living creature over the bridge. My friends told me when the invisible strings are cut off and you don't move, you deserve and get the "swallowing up rule." In fact I don't know what happens next. I just know when one of my old owner's invisible strings was cut off and she was not able to move anymore, the devil doppelganger swallowed her."

Charli looked so sad and miserable. He went to Nana. Nana bent over and pet him. She said: "Oh, little cute dog! I'll stay always with you. I promise!" Then she stood up and said: "Now let's go. We should not stop here — don't forget the rules."

They all set out. Nana thought of a rule thata was not mentioned by Charlie; the rule of crossing! You should be swallowed by the iron gate to start a life here on the bridge. Rule number zero.

CHAPTER 4

The House

Apana, the ever-young sister of the family, sat on the gable roof of the house and said something in the ear of the house that made it laugh slowly. Nana was vacuuming the house because she believed that untidiness and dust could stop the regulation of good energy. Perhaps keeping the house clean was a grateful response to the security the house brought them. Anyway, the house was ticklish, so it was easier for Apana to make the house to laugh when Nana was vacuuming. Charlie was afraid of the vacuum cleaner, and it was the only time he left his role as Nana's shadow-like follower; he turned around and watched her from a distance. It was an interesting and funny scene for Apana and Nana's little son, Dara, to get entertained.

After cleaning the house, Nana made tea for herself while she was enjoying the beautiful circulation of energy within the house. Apana sat on one of the cherry tree branches while moving her legs freely around and trying on her cherry earrings. The house slowly thanked Nana with love. Nana smiled with satisfaction and took her cup of tea in her hands. She remembered the first day she met the house. On those days, the house was old, worn out, abandoned and on the verge of being swallowed. The beginning of the friendship between Nana and the house was an amazing story that showed a caring presence of someone in her life. That happening was an invisible and pragmatic attention of a higher power that made Nana believe she was not left alone and forgotten. A protection that made it easier to tolerate her suffering and loneliness on the bridge. They had found each other at their crossing point when Nana was getting away from the iron gate and moving forward. The house was going backwards because it was not able to move on the bridge and it was left on its own. It was at that crossing point that the house made its last try and asked Nana to wish for it deep from her heart. Nana, who was seeking shelter, closed her eyes and wished for the house deep from her heart. In a special moment when strange music could be heard, she felt the invisible strings of the house were put into her hands. When she opened her eyes, she saw the rusty and old keys of the house in her hands. After that they had belonged together.

CHAPTER 5

Just One Day to Love

There was a fuss and uproar in the house. Apana and Charlie were running around and laughing. As soon as Nana arrived at the house, she quickly ran to the windows and closed them. When all the curtains were still in front of the windows, Charlie and Apana got quiet too. Silence reigned in the house. Suddenly a continuous tap tap sound could be heard coming from the kitchen. They went there to see what was going on. It was a dragonfly who was not able to understand the nature of the glass. It wanted to escape from the house. Apana stretched out her hand and took its glassy and elegant wings. The dragonfly looked at her with his big round eyes and said: "Let me go!"

Apana asked curiously: "Are you in hurry?"

The dragonfly replied: "Yes, I have to go and find other dragonflies to make babies for our species to continue. You know what? My life as a dragonfly is as long as the passage of the sun from the east to the west. I just live from a sunrise to a sunset. There is no tomorrow for me. I have just one day to love. Charlie was next to Apana and listening.

He asked: "Just one day?? You cannot be grown up in a day, can you?"

The dragonfly answered: "I've spent three years deep under the water of lagoons. Today I tore my worm-shaped body and came out. Now in my new shape as a dragonfly, I have just one day to make a life full of love."

Apana asked: "And then?"

Dragonfly said: "Then my heart stops beating; in other words, I die."

Apana wondered: "My heart doesn't beat but I am not dead."

The little dragonfly paused a bit then said: "Well, to be 'alive' and to 'live' are the most complicated words in the world. Maybe it's better to find out the meaning of death. Static, steady, motion also has interwoven meanings."

Nana, standing by the window, was the witness of the conversation while she was watching the apple tree. Its leaves were pale and yellow and some had fallen at the foot of the tree. Autumn could be felt, the invisible strings of time.

The dragonfly continued: "For example, these yellow leaves used to be green one day. Now if these leaves stay green forever, don't they have some from of stillness and death? Wouldn't it look like they have no life, like rocks and mountains? However, our lives are so short compared to mountains and deserts. We cannot understand their changes and vitality. But in the geographic memory of time, there were many deserts that used to be seas and valleys that were mountains. My life is a day long in your calendar, but for me it is a life long. Now if I find another dragonfly and fly passionately with her, my life is worth a century. On the other hand, if we spend our time happily, our lives will be as short as a blink of an eye."

Then he looked at Apana and said: "Up to my calendar, I have been kept a week in your hand. Can you release me?"

Apana responded with embarrassment: "Sorry, I was distracted. For me the invisible strings of time have been cut a long time ago. I am like memories which through the time and mind go on but I don't become old and I don't change."

Charlie grumbled to himself. He could not understand them. He lazily went to a corner and put his head on his paws for a nap.

Nana opened the window and the dragonfly and Apana flew out of the window happily. Apana joyfully chased the dragonfly to witness his new friend's one-day love life. Life and death and the intertwining of these worlds. Nana found herself like the little prince of her favorite book who was only responsible for the selfish red rose and the two dormant volcanoes. To find her answers, she would undoubtedly have to leave her little planet. This journey had begun a long time ago.

CHAPTER 6

Silence is the Beginning of Hearing

Wind didn't have good news. The two apple and cherry trees were chattering in each other's ears. The news was about Apana, the ever-young sister of the family. It was about a long time ago when Apana's invisible strings had not been cut off, about the time that she was not everlasting and she was an ordinary person. It was about the time that she used to live in the snowy land. That was when Nana had recently moved into the house and there was a long distance between her and the snowy land. Nana had to go there.

It was a journey that was possible with the help of migrant white geese. The first step was to have a strong desire and wish, so, as the house had taught her, she closed her eyes and wished that she could see her sister. she hasn't seen Apana for a long time. Her heart was always filled with the hope of a sweet visit. The hope that could be in vain with that terrible news. Her heart was swinging like a metal ball between the fire of will and the coldness of the fear. That made it difficult for her to concentrate on her wish. Whatever it was, she was able to put all her power in her turbulent heart to make a miracle come true.

After awhile, the two trees called her. A group of wild geese were flying above their heads. The sky was partly cloudy but just before disappearing behind a piece of the cloud, one of the geese turned and flew towards Nana. Charlie was barking while he was looking at the sky. His guardian instincts forced him to react to the slightest possible danger. Nana told him: "Be quiet dear Charlie! It is coming here for me, I called it."

But Charlie didn't stop barking. The white goose landed on the balcony of the house despite the dog's warning. It was bigger than how it looked in the sky. It extended its neck to Charlie and said: "Didn't you hear what Nana told you? Quiet!"

Charlie turned to Nana in fear and wagged his tail. Nana caressed him kindly. With it's odd voice, the goose told Charlie: "Silence little dog. Don't you know that silence is the beginning of hearing?"

Any time Charlie couldn't figure something out, he would get a stupid and funny look on his face. He glanced at them with bewilderment.

The goose continued: "Yes, silence is the beginning of hearing. The voice of the heart is the voice of silence. It is in absolute silence that ghosts and waves are starting to dance. Music pieces are written and poetry and arts are born. When all the sounds go to sleep, such words wake up that were lost in the chaos of the mind. You are able to hear the sounds that are telling stories from a hidden part of your soul. It's the voice of our moods, decisions and inspirations. The voices that can not be heard in the chaos of life. Silence is good. Silence is always good.

Charlie sighed: "Dear goose, I am a very quiet dog. Most of the time I stay alone at home without any words but I didn't hear or feel any of the things you have mentioned."

The goose waved his neck and said: "But silence is not about being quiet and not speaking. Silence means absolute inner stillness. Chaos is against silence, and stillness defeats chaos. Loneliness and having nobody to talk, does not mean there is a silence. Silence is the quietness of the mind. In fact that is the thought which must be quiet. After that your heart starts to speak. All the irony and suffering shows the beautiful sides of themselves, and love can be seen through them. All human beings' naggings change to beautiful music. The heart finds a chance to reveal its beauty and awareness. The heart says: 'Watch me!' and when you are the guest of silence, you get excited in the celebration of all the untouched beauty. All the pain and suffering is replaced by the absolute inner beauty."

Charlie listened disappointedly and said: "I always pray and hope for Nana's return in when I am alone and wait for her. But nothing happens. How was it possible that you were able to hear Nana from that far distance and come to her?"

Goose answered: "There is a difference between hope and faith. Waiting and hoping have the sense of the future and they feed the mind. But faith means to live in the present time. Faith is the language of the heart. Oh dear Charlie, you know what! Once all the hearts were in fact a part of a complete mirror of existence. But for some reason that mirror was broken to thousands of pieces and every piece took a place in a heart. All the hearts with too many different invisible strings are connected and feel each other. In the silence of the mind, all the hearts became one and are able to visit each other and heal each other while their owners are not aware of it. It is not possible that a heart suffers and the world of beauty does not suffer. In the world of silence, nobody is alone or strange. We are the roots of one tree in the name of existence. For us as the white geese, flying so long causes us to hear the sounds of hearts more easily because of our silence." Then it turned to Nana and said: "I am at your service dear Nana!" It opened its wings and said: "Get on! It is time for another journey."

CHAPTER 7

Emancipation

Nana, now on the back of the goose, saw her belongings, her son, her man, Charlie and the house, the apple and the cherry trees all disappearing. The cold wind wrapped around her hair but the warmth of the goose's body gave her comfort and relief. Flying — what a wonderful pleasure! Her body was weightless and her soul was free. From above everything seemed small and insignificant. Houses, the city and even the bridge.

Nana started a conversation with the goose: "How is that you can fly?"

The goose answered: "Emancipation and liberation from whatever exists and does not exist. What exists means the concrete world, and nonexistence means those that are just in our illusioned minds. Flying is a suspension among everything between the Earth and the sky, mobility and immobility, hope and disparity. Flying means to be free from everything. And this a lesson that the sea can teach you. A swimmer should let himself be free in the nature of the water. He must trust the nature of the water and just give up struggling, which means to die somehow, to not be a stranger to the water and be immersed freely. Then you are able to swim and the water makes you float. What I mean is to change the level of your consciousness to unconsciousness. After all, you can choose what to do and where to go. Then you can choose to be like a fish or a drop of rain.

"There is the same story for the birds. As long as they do not jump down in a deep and terrifying valley, as long as they do not experience the falling and not opening their wings like a 'cross' as a sign of surrender, they can never ride the wind and fly. First they must be one with the nature of the wind to get high. But I tell you what: emancipation is in fact 'the love' itself. It means to return to your beginning, to experience paradise but this time with awareness. So I think the key of flying and achieving is emancipation."

CHAPTER 8

Names

As the geese gradually climbed in the sky, the feeling of anxiousness and dependence gave way to emancipation and lightness.

Nana asked the Goose: "By the way, what is your name?"

The goose answered: "We have no name. Down there when you look up at our group, what you see is a group of migrating white geese, like drops in the sea. There is no drop, it is the sea. At that height we have no identity other than the group. We are one in our group, we cannot have a name when we all have the same goal, which is to get to our destination without competing.

"Naming is your weird human habit. It divides and discriminates. You want to give an identity by naming everything around in order to remind yourself that they are something other than you, so you are able to own them. This strange habit keeps you at humanistic levels. Inside societies, metropolises and cities, there are millions upon millions of unknown units; like a labyrinth for your mankind. Imagine what could have happened to the colonies of ants and bees if they had this strange habit. Their society could never have any harmony or cooperation."

Nana was quietly thinking about herself, her family, Charlie; each of them was a world in a bigger world. Each of them had their own story.

The white goose added: "And you know, dear Nana, this specific nature of the human being, I mean giving identity and names to everything, is very contagious. Everyone and everything in contact with you can have an impact. Look, I am a goose in my group, but by your side I am 'the goose Nana is riding.' You discriminate between everything so seriously and inevitably that you can't imagine anything else. Look! From here above can you see borderlines? The borderlines that you have drawn on your geography maps and books? You've created flags for your lands and waged wars over and make believe the imaginary borderlines and prejudice.

"Look at the forests — which tree? Or the seas — which drop? Listen to the symphony of the universe! Everyone and everything has a part in it. They are fault-free and harmonious. All of us are a part of this symphony, the symphony of universe."

Padid Tree*

At that height on the white goose, it was cold and still. Nana gradually fell asleep. The cold seeped into her veins like a deadly poison and was quietly freezing her blood. Nana had a strange dream. It began on a warm night. The window was open. The light blue curtains were dancing gently with the breeze that was blowing in. The moonlight was shining through like a magic whisper. Suddenly, Charlie (that slept next to Nana's feet) moved and sharpened his ears. There was magic everywhere. Cracks appeared in the front wall. Charlie growled in his throat and was on high alert. Through the cracks came some roots of a tree that were searching all around. Charlie got ready to bark and awaken Nana, but like an old man's hand, one of the roots invited him to be quiet. A deep, familiar and kind voice of a man said: "Shhhh ... I am her."

---

*Padid in Farsi means "emerge"

Charlie had no choice but to obey. The dancing roots reached to Nana's toes, then slowly entered into Nana's veins. The nectar inside the roots warmed Nana's frozen blood. Nana opened her eyes. Her eyes had the color of rapture and dream. The roots went up her from her feet and then towards the legs and thighs. Gently her abdomen, belly, chest and the whole body were covered by the roots. Then Nana found herself in a green and bright land. The roots of Padid tree had no limitations in time or place. Wherever and whenever they wanted, they were able to be there. There was a huge forest in front of her. The trees whispered in her ears. There was an excitement in the air; some jealously, some eagerly and some passionately looked at her. There were some branches that guided her toward Padid tree with great envy. Now it was just Nana and Padid tree. Nana embraced the shining trunk of the tree and the tree impatiently cuddled her. A magnificent tango began. The springs of love flowed and watered the trees.

A cheerful celebration began. The nectar of Padid tree was in fact the essence of Nana's life. What Padid tree had given her during those long years, made Nana be able to run her life. The tree whose fruits were poems and its leaves had the smell of the nirvana ocean. Sometimes they traveled to the Taj Mahal, or sometimes they read Khayyam's quatrains on the great pyramids of Egypt. Sometimes they experienced a primitive life in an ancient cave or danced by the raging flames of fire of the Spanish gypsies. Sometimes they were in the Himalayas with a hermit in an abandoned temple and sometimes in a cozy tea house in Haraz Road in Chaloos with a warm drink. Nana narrated the heavenly worlds of her dreams and the tree composed the most romantic poems of its own. Padid tree owed its thousand-year age to her and Nana owed her existence to him. What man can call 'coexist,' love or eternity.

Trees are the ministrants of travelers and pilgrims who are seeking consciousness and awareness. Trees are the start point of Buddha and prophets in their spiritual journey and wayfaring.

The dance finished. The life nectar of the tree removed the coldness from her veins. The trees were singing: "Tomorrow we will be born again, tomorrow we will be born again!" The voices and images were intertwined. The geese were screaming to give a massage loud enough to awaken Nana. From above, the snowy land could be seen.

CHAPTER 10

Jump Down!

Nana, who was euphoric and confused about her dream, asked: "Dear goose, what are your friends saying?"

The goose replied: "They say, 'Jump down!'"

Nana's eyes rounded with surprise and she asked: "What? Jumping from this high?"

Goose confirmed.

"But why?"

"If you don't jump now, it will happen in your life as your destiny."

"And how do I know this is a correct message?"

"Because it comes from those ones who have no benefit in it. Now choose! Either avoid or trust!"

Nana could not see any choice in the message. But according to what the goose told her, that day or later it could come to her once again. There was no option. Nana hesitated for a while. She could hear different voices in her head. An inner seductive voice told her: "ump Nana!, a miracle might happen and you could survive, you may get two wings or something". It was a deceiving voice that encouraged her to have faith. But there was another voice that was the opposite. The voice told her. Be wise and realistic! Why should a miracle happen? There are reasons for things to happen, the facts, how a is it possible to be survive after jumping down from that high, there is no chance, be wise"

These dialogues continued in her head but after a while she liked the seductive voice. She had to be brave and made her choice as she stepped out for the journey. So in an insane moment, she opened her arms and left the goose's neck and jumped down.

CHAPTER 11

Balance

Nana was swirling and falling down like a leaf in the wind. The fear overcame her, and she realized the absurdity of the voice that had promised her two wings. There was no miracle. Fear had conquered all of her soul and body. The world was slowly darkening before her eyes. Helplessly, her hands were trying to grab the air, and her eyes searched anxiously for help. There was a sudden pain and she just switched off like a TV.

She opened her eyes with great shock and found herself not on the ground but on the white goose's back. "Did I see a dream?" Nana asked breathlessly.

"No, you experienced perception," said the goose.

"And what was it?" Nana asked.

Goose answered with a question: "What was the last thing you saw?"

"Nothing," Nana thoughtfully replied.

The goose asked: "And did you get the message?"

Nana was quiet.

"Dear Nana, this terrible fall had a beautiful message for you. 'Balance.' Remember that waiting for a miracle or having a pair of wings is fascinating, but you cannot ignore the realities. This is the message. Keep heaven and Earth always in balance and you will reach your destination."

CHAPTER 12

The Heart of a Lion or the Spirit of a Wolf

When she arrived in the snowy land, she said goodbye to the geese. A heavy snow and blizzard welcomed her. What was she doing there? What was she going to look for? What was the next step? No address, no way to get in touch, and worst of all, she had lost her sense of navigation. Where was Apana? The massive volume of anxiousness pushed her away from her conscious nature ... looking for a sign, she was staring into in the darkness. Her fingertips were getting colder and colder and then her hands. She was full of fear and frustration. Suddenly, in the darkness, she saw two burning fires coming towards her. There was little hope in her heart, but they were not fire. They were two bright eyes of a white wolf that was looking at her. A native man was riding on a sleigh the wolf was pulling.

The native man said: "Welcome to the snowy land 'lion-hearted lady'! But what you need here is not the heart of a desert lion, you need the spirit of a snowy land wolf."

He knew what was going to happen to her. Every land demands its own tool for life. The white wolf put his head in Nana's ice-covered hands. Nana bent over and caressed him. Dogs and wolves were once family too. But little Charlie and the wolf had nothing in common, especially the wolf's eyes and gaze. There was an irrepressible and wild force in the wolf's eyes that awakened Nana's instincts. Might be there was once a common root or sprite between Nana and the wolf. The blood surged through her veins faster and she gnashed her teeth in rage. The great and fighting spirit of the wolf gradually conquered her soul. So that was all she needed because a war was on the way. Pointing at Nana, the native man told her to sit down beside him in the sleigh. He covered Nana with a wolf skin and said: "Let's go to the Hotel of God"

CHAPTER 13

The Hotel of God*

Nana knew that ever since she was swallowed by the iron gate and until she reached that land, there were invisible strings that were unjustifiable and undeniable. Endeavor is sometimes the most useless thing in the world. From the beginning of her journey on the bridge she had realized that she had to go alone on the great river of fate and be patient, silent and empty, so that the world could reflect on it in a proper way. It was just like that unique flake of snow melting in her hands at the beginning of the bridge.

The Hotel of God was a sanctuary that was in fact the last patients' station. The Hotel of God was the place where many miracles took place. Hotel of God was a place where she could meet her Apana. On that snowy night, Nana was hopeful, determined and eager when she arrived at the Hotel of God.

---

* Hôtel-Dieu de Montréal (literally translated as The House of God) is a special cancer hospital in Quebec City.

CHAPTER 14

Nest of Ants

The Hotel of God was like a nest of ants. Nurses, doctors and staff ... were a community. Their endless shifts were like a running stream. People were replaced by other people but the duties went on day and night. Nurses of different shifts, whoever they were, did their routine with a smile on their faces. Pills, ampoules and food. There were also irregular shifts of patients too. One patient stayed for a few days and then another ... just like worn and damaged parts of machines that were repaired in factories. Other parts of the hospital, such as the accounting department, insurance and pharmacy were no exception. Everything was done in an automated and planned way. It was like other hospitals: soulless, lifeless and sometimes horrible.

Nana was very sad. Finding Apana in the colony of ants was not an easy task. The one who she was looking for played an important role in Nana's identity and life. Apana was lost somewhere in that labyrinth named the 'Hotel of God.'

Apana

Nana remembered George Orwell's novel. The number of files was more valid than the names of the people. The hospital receptionist could not find Apana by her name, and she even doubted that such a patient could be there. Nana insisted and that made the staff of hospital search more. She waited off to the side for a while. She was feeling so bad about the cool indifference the staff had about her sister. Apana was not a number, she was a lost human being in Nana's world. Nana was on fire; an angry wolf was howling inside her. But she tried to sit still and follow the things that the house taught her about wishing and hoping. She tried again.

She shut her eyes and called Apana: "Here I am Apana, please find me."

A tear rolled from her eye. How close and how far. Every prayer got an answer somehow so a young nurse came up to her and took her to a room. Nana could have sworn at that time, her heart, her dreams and her life had stopped for a while. She could not believe her eyes.

Again the wolf was howling inside her, but her face was determined, kind and strong. She went towards Apana and embraced that slender, lean body: "It's over. I've got you. I'll never let you go again."

That moment was indescribable.

CHAPTER 16

Repetition of the Childhood

They were together again just like their childhood. Nana was not with her family, neither was Apana at her job. Once there in hospital, again it was not important, neither the place, nor the time or what Mom was cooking for lunch.

When they were children, they used to spend hours together observing the world beyond the limits and laws of their land. Like two old astronomers with their primitive telescopes, they had been able to watch the infinite space from that tiny little eyepiece. And they had been the first people to find out that the sun did not rotate around the earth, but on the contrary, it was the earth that orbited the sun, and so they had been cursed by their society and despised. Those two shoulder-to-shoulder leaders had been like the female wolves who didn't want to be domesticated by the leir and hypocritical shepherds. In fact, they were again the same children who were playing the role of adults and they had a chance to be together until the end of one of them.

CHAPTER 17

The Forty Stories

The pain ran through Apana's body. Four doctors met Nana around Apana's bed that night. And in the cruelty of honesty they told Apana that she would not stay so long. It might be the next day or forty nights later; they didn't know for sure.

An intense silence enveloped the two sisters' souls. But it wasn't time to be scared and hopeless, or to mourn. Now it was the time to fight back and resist.

Nana broke the silence and said, "Have you ever heard the story 'It's Too Late'?"

"No, how does it go? Does it help?"

Nana said: "Apana! Stories are sometimes more enjoyable than life itself."

The most unique characteristic of humans is imagination. It is the *one* that other creatures probably lack. In the world of imagination, the uglies can be seen as beautiful, the nightmares can become sweet dreams *and* elephants can dance *or* rhinos can fly. You can take the hand of your beloved when it would not be possible in the real world. You can be a satisfied devil or a regretful angel, a worm or a butterfly, or a walnut tree over a hill. Oh Apana, without imagination there would be no art, no poetry. One can not forget the enormous pain of *life* without his imagination ... so give me your hand and come with me to the land of the stories. And let's imagine the stories to escape from the real world. To stop this pain until the miracle can happen to us."

It was a good offer. Nana took Apana's hand in hers and said: "Well, let me start with 'It's Too Late.'"

Then, like a child, Apana shifted her head on the pillow and settled in to listen. She looked at Nana with a glinting eye.

It's Too Late

Nana asked: "Have you ever heard a melodic story?"

Apana shook her head.

Nana explained: "Imagine background music and continue while I am telling you the story. In this story things are dance-like and musical; it is better for more joy."

Then she paused for some seconds and gave Apana a little time to concentrate.

So she started the story: Once upon a time, there was a man who was sleeping under a tree. Where or under which tree? I don't know, and it is not important. He woke up when a light beam shone on his face through the branches of the tree that he slept under. The sweet and cheerful sound of birds could be heard. He got up halfway. He didn't know where he was. Was it a dream? Not sure. He just felt delighted and free. He heard a singing song. It was so heartwarming that the young man forgot his questions and curiosity. He went after to find the owner of that magnificent female sound. Shortly thereafter he saw a young woman sitting and making a crown with flowers. She was so beautiful that the young man fell in love at first glance. When she added the last flower to her crown she put it in her long hair and twisted ... and sang a happier song than before. She walked towards the young man who was hiding behind a tree and watching her. She reached out to him as if she already knew where he was.

"What is your name?" the man asked.

"Violet, and you?"

The man answered: "I can't remember."

Ignoring his answer, Violet offered her hand to the young man. The man hesitantly took it. At the same time, happy music was heard and they started dancing and roaming the beautiful garden until they reached out to a group of young girls who were just as beautiful as his Violet. It was just like a garden full of beautiful flowers. The girls called each other in different flower names.

Suddenly a trumpet was heard and everyone was silent. That made the young man be quiet too. Then the girls stood in two rows facing each other. Shortly afterwards two girls brought a rug and opened it on the ground and placed a beautiful chair in the middle. Then a woman entered whose beauty could mock the beauty of the moon and the sun. She sat down on the chair charmingly. The young man had never experienced such charisma in his life. At once he forgot his beautiful sweetheart and his newfound love. He was in love deeply with the prettiest woman he had ever seen. The flower crowned Violet became so sad. She knew their love was over and now her beloved's heart was attracted to another. A tear rolled from her eye and she sang a sad song. The song affected the beautiful lady, so she stood up and ordered the man to be thrown out of the garden. The young man fell down at the lady's feet and begged for forgiveness.

"I had never tasted such sweet love in my life," he said.

The beautiful woman said, "Love? All men say the same thing, but if they find a more beautiful one, they leave it and go to the new one."

"Oh, I'm not like others. It's true that I liked the girl in the flower crown, but when I saw you I realized you were my true love and I'll love you forever and ever."

The beautiful woman said, "How do I know you're a true lover?"

The man said, "I will do whatever you want me to do."

The pretty lady pointed and one of the girls brought an ebony black box and opened it and stood beside her.

The young woman looked into the box and asked, "Anything I want?"

The man said, "Yes. I'll even give you my life; a lover has nothing more important than his life."

She grabbed a dagger which was in the box and lifted it up and plunged it right into the young man's heart. With disbelief, the man put his hand on his chest and died while looking at her with eyes full of love. The woman turned around and said, "He was really in love but so what! Anyway it's too late." And she left the garden. The end.

For a moment the two sisters had forgotten where they were and why. A nurse came into the room. According to the doctor's prescription, she added some painkiller to Apana's serum and said goodnight and returned to her ant-like colony.

"Why did you kill the young man in your story?" Apana asked.

"He was himself the cause of his death. I was just the narrator."

"But when men, like the one in your story, see a better woman and leave their spouses it's by bad luck there is always one better."

Then they both laughed at the irony because they both knew the story wasn't about men and women, it was about the inevitable part of humanity: "It's Too Late."

Nana kissed Apana's forehead. She felt like she was stabbed in the heart remembering the doctor's words about Apana's fatal disease. How many nights would Apana have left?

Nana hushed her thoughts, returned to her chair and watched Apana. She waited until Apana went to sleep, just like a mother looking after her child.

CHAPTER 19

The Roots of Palid Tree*

Nana was just falling asleep as she felt a burning in her toes. She opened her eyes. Some black roots were touching her leg. She was frightened and pulled herself back. She glanced at Apana and saw another black root around her sister's hand. Angrily and instinctively, she rushed to the black root and snatched it, which was like a black snake, and threw it to a corner. The roots went back to the hole that they had come out of and disappeared. Everything calmed down again. There was no sign of the roots or the hole. Apana was bleeding from the needle of her serum. Nana called the nurse. The nurse came and replaced the needle. Nana looked worried about what had happened. In silence she watched Apana.

It was morning and she could not sleep. Apana opened her eyes. She looked exhausted and pale.

---

* In Farsi, Palid means someone or something evil.

She smiled and asked Nana: "You didn't sleep last night, did you?"

Nana smiled as she remembered what had happened last night. Then Apana told her about her nightmare. About a black snake around her body. Nana told her not to be worried because it was just a nightmare.

A nurse came to take a daily morning test sample.

Nana thought of the black roots. Her toes were still burning. The fear took over her. She had to stay awake from that night on to find out what it was.

CHAPTER 20

Today's Children, Yesterday's Children

Breakfast was brought to Apana. Black coffee and wheat porridge. Nana pushed the bedside table in front of Apana and pressed the automatic button beside the bed, lifting Apana's so she could sit up. It would hurt a lot, but the painkillers were a big help. Apana asked as she dipped her spoon into her porridge: "By the way, didn't your little son get upset that you went away?"

"Well, no, not at all. When he found out I'm coming to help you, he became happy."

In the silence, there were lots of words that remained unsaid. But the eyes couldn't lie, so they tried to get engaged in something to avoid eye contact. Apana with her spoon and Nana with bedding on Apana's feet.

Nana said: "We are lucky to have each other. Yesterday's kids were happier than today's kids, don't you think so?"

"How?"

"Today's world is full of so many unknown lands and fields of science. Medicine, psychology, sociology but they are not happier people than we used to be. I remember that in our time there were no such scientific titles but everything was in order. Our neighbors were part of our family but they lived just a wall away. You knew that the intimacy, the innocence, and the simplicity of our souls sweetened the taste of our tea beside the simple bread and cheese in those days.

"But now, everything has progressed ... developed ... along with the distance between our next door neighbors. The thickness of our neighbors' walls has increased too. I live there and you live here far from all ... We were not as wealthy as my son — little Dara — but we were happier for sure."

Apana was looking at the sunrise. She could still remember the sweetness of her childhood. Nana was right. Today's children, despite everything they have, are much lonelier than the children of yesterday. She remembered their first real doll and asked Nana: "Do you remember Nazi?"

Nana smiled and nodded: "Yes, Nazi, a doll for two little girls. It belonged to us, we never thought who had a larger share of it. It just belonged to us. Whatever we decided about her there was no fight, there was never something in the name of 'mine or yours' and we never asked or complained for another one. Such a unique world."

Then both sighed thinking what really happened to that world, to those simple and happy children, family, neighbors and people. When or where they had really lost that paradise. Now they were again together, just like their childhood.

CHAPTER 21

The Broken Wings

It was the next day, and the sun was slowly conquering the sky with its soft glow. Two birds danced in the sky. The two sisters were in their cage of the hospital room and were watching the birds. Both of them had a smile on their lips. Suddenly, Nana remembered something and sighed.

Apana asked: "How is our bird man?"

Nana sighed again and said: "He is the bravest man I know. Starting a new life from the bottom of a black hole with the name of destiny is very difficult. Although he is no longer able to fly, he has never forgotten the sky and he hasn't given up to the darkness. He is not an ordinary man and you know that flying is an eternal spell. My man is no exception. To be half a bird and half a man without his iron wings is always painful for him. He will never forget the wings he was forced to leave behind the iron gate. Before starting our journey over the bridge, we were hoping to have the wings with us, but — as you know, Apana — everything has a price. His wings were the price of our decision to leave our land to find a better place for us and a better sky to fly in. You know it was not possible for us to live in that dark and smoky sky of our homeland anymore. We needed a better land with clear blue skies not just for ourselves but also as responsible parents of our little Dara. We didn't know we'd have to pay a lot for that. Now we have the blue sky, but we don't have many things, such as his wings. Sometimes I can hear his iron wings cry behind the iron gate. But there was no other choice; he could not bring them, but he promised them and himself that one day he would reclaim them. In fact, I hear the cry from many of those things and people we have left behind. But what else could we do? We couldn't tolerate that dark, smoky land. It was too dark for us. We have to accept the facts too."

"Was it that simple?" Apana asked.

"No, not at all, it wasn't easy at all," Nana said. "I still see wounds on my man's shoulders; sometimes they bleed and make his shirt bloody. My man sometimes doesn't want me to see his face in pain so he sleeps with his back to me. He forgets that the language of the heart cannot be heard by the ears. I feel his pain and I turn my back on him while I cry for his lost wings and our lost land. Whatever he is, he is half human and half bird."

A nurse came into the room to check something and they never spoke of this topic again. There through the window, an airplane could be seen with two iron wings.

The Ladybird Lady

After breakfast and regular visits by doctors and nurses, the two sisters found a chance to relax again.

Apana asked Nana: "What are you doing in your new land?"

Nana said, "Now I am teaching, but at the beginning I used to help the 'Ladybird Lady.'"

Apana's eyes grew wide and she asked with surprise: "Ladybird Lady? What do you mean?"

"Well, that means a woman who is a ladybird." Nana bent over to Apana and slowly whispered in her ear: "It's actually a secret that I discovered a while ago. If I tell you, will you please keep it as our secret?"

Apana said: "Okay, I'll do it."

Nana smiled and continued: "Well, in our neighborhood lives a woman who is 100 years old. She's a bit egoistic and selfish. She lives in a big house and still loves sweets and behaves like a young woman in love. She loves dresses, colors and handsome men."

"What a great old lady! Such a spirit is adorable."

"Dear me, I learned a lot from her. For example, she taught me that age isn't just numbers. Feeling young is in your heart and it doesn't matter how old you are. But what makes this neighbor lady special to me is that she's not really a human, she's a ladybird."

Apana was surprised and as usual lifted her eyebrows thoughtfully and looked at Nana carefully: "Tell me exactly what she looks like so I can get the idea!"

"Well, you know ladybirds are solitary and not very sociable insects. You rarely see two or three of them together in a place. I've never seen them as a colony in my entire life. I found it curious that she collected them in a corner by the window."

"Oh!"

"Well, sometimes when I watered the pots, the corners of the window were full of dead and dying ladybirds. I noticed that the old lady got touchy when I went near them or got mad if I wanted to touch them. Once she told me angrily not to go there anymore. The old lady hates spiders just like ladybirds and also you can't find any spiders in her house. She is a very clean woman, so why did she love having so many dead and dying insects? Weird habits. And else, there were always so many ladybirds."

Apana nodded her head in agreement, but deep in her heart she knew how much Nana had suffered working for the old woman It was Nana's strange habit to change the bitter and sad experiences to the sweet imaginary games of fantasy with her creative and unique mind. It was the same for Apana. She had the same ability. Apana used to call her boy friend "Lion" and her boy friend used to call Apana "Gazelle." It was a sad love story of a hunter and a hunted Using her body in a sudden instinct hunger and leaving her heart untouched, Games of mind turn the bitters to sweet, the story of the ladydird lady or the lion and Gazelle were true and also no true.

CHAPTER 23

What Does God Look Like?

It was a quiet night. The two sisters were enjoying the miracle of being together. The insidious pain made Apana impatient, so to start a conversation and forget the pain, she asked Nana: "What does God look like?"

Nana thought a little and said: "This question reminds me of a story. Do you want to hear it?"

Apana nodded.

Nana started: "Once upon a time, a rural woman went to the spring to fill her jug with water for home use because at that time there was no tap water in her village. She was tired and sighed: "Ahh." Suddenly, a young man appeared in front of her. She was frightened and asked him who he was. The boy introduced himself as 'Ahh' and asked the woman why she called him. She remembered a moment ago that she was filling her jug and had sighed. She was very tired and wished she could have some rest. He heard that and smiled and disappeared. She thought she might have been dreaming, so she took her jug and went back home.

It was a hot summer evening and the woman had to go to the roof to prepare the mosquito net for sleeping at night. But she fell down the stairs and broke one of her legs. After a month she recovered and was able to walk and work. One morning she sighed again and the young man appeared to her again. Ahh asked what was wrong with her and she told him that breaking her leg what not exactly what she meant when she asked for 'rest.' Ahh replied that she would not remember that the woman had clarified exactly what she meant except the word 'rest.' So this time the woman wished to receive some beautiful and precious gifts and that nothing unpleasant would happen. Ahh smiled and went.

The next day some uninvited guests came to her home with lots of precious and beautiful gifts and souvenirs. Although the gifts pleased the rural woman a lot and made her happy, the guests stayed with her for a month and the woman had to cater to them day and night. Apart from how tired she was, she spent a great deal of money on feeding the guests. After their departure, the angry woman sat in a corner of the room and sighed. When Ahh appeared this time, the rural women was furious and explained that the details didn't work at all, she had suffered even more. The woman also told Ahh that she was afraid of wishing because there was always something wrong with her wishes. So she wished to be the same simple woman again and be happy for what might come. After that she never sighed and never saw Ahh again.

Apana smiled and said, "Nana, do you think our God is what we imagine?"

"Exactly. He is exactly as we would like to be, and always imperfectly," Nana said.

This was their last conversation about God. The question "what God looks like" was forever replaced by just simply accepting God as it was accepted by the human beings and ancestors centuries ago: as a pure source of unknown power who grants their wishes. God was who he should be. He was the one as well as he was no one.

CHAPTER 24

The Great Div and the little Dive*

Watching the snow fall behind the hospital window could have been spectacular as the two sympathetic sisters waited together for Apana's healing and deliverance from that sad place.

Nana asked Apana: "When did your pain start?"

"It is not easy to believe it," said Apana, "but what I want to say right now is exactly what had happened." And then she looked at Nana sadly.

Nana understood what she meant and said, "Dear Apana, don't worry. I know the world is full of weird things. Whether you believe in them or not, they exist. So don't worry; tell me what's in your heart!"

---

* A Div is an imaginary creature in old Iranian stories. They are comparable to demons or giants.

Apana agreed and began: "One night on my first days of my stays here, on a cold and snowy night, I was awakened by a strange sound. I was scared of what I saw. I wanted to scream. But I was unable to move. I could see, feel and hear, but I couldn't move. Do you know what I saw?"

Nana shook her head.

"I saw two 'Divs.' They were standing next to my bed. One big and one small. They were speaking in a language that I could not understand. Then the little Dive jumped on my belly and started jumping up and down. The bigger one was trying to stop the little one. Although I couldnt undrestand their language, I could feel the bigger on was trying to stop him. But the little Dive did not listen to him and continoued jumping until he finally pushed himself into my abdomen. I was overwhelmed with the pain that was writhing in me, and I fainted. I thought I was unconscious all night because it was morning when I woke up."

Nana looked at Apana;remembering once facing a Div, that she had never talked about him to any one.

"I saw them, Nana. Do you think I dreamed it?" A glance of excitement in her eyes begged Nana.

Nana asked: "So this little Div or whatever, is the cause of your illness, right?"

Apana answered: "I think so. After that night I have never felt healthy. But Nana, who believes me? The world is full of one-dimensional things and realities, but I'm a creature with different dimensions, and these facts don't fit together."

Nana said: "Well, after starting my life on the bridge and noticing the existence of invisible strings of laws in the world of 'to be or not to be,' I think nothing is impossible. Maybe a land of 'Divs' exists. Who knows? But dear Apana, we will take you out. We pray together and make faith. When the snow melts, I promise to get you out of here. We will stay together and forever."

The nurse came into the room and changed Apana's serum. Nana remembered the black roots. What they were. What was happening. Everything seemed unknown and mysterious. A wolf inside her soul was warning her of something she could not understand. It was snowing so heavily and cruelly.

C H A P T E R   2 5

Camisado

nother night came with more pain killers for a better sleep. But Nana waited. She knew something was going to happen. She sat motionless on her chair and stared into the corner of the wall where the black roots had disappeared. Hours passed and Nana fell asleep unwillingly.

"Get out of the room, Nana. Get out of the room." It was the familiar but alarming voice of Padid tree. Nana opened her eyes and looked at Apana. There were so many black roots around her body. She attacked the roots and tried to push them away from her sister with her bare hands. She felt a severe burning when she touched them, but her protective instinct overwhelmed the pain. Then she felt the roots of Padid tree around her waist trying to pull her out of the dangerous battle.

"Release it Nana, there's nothing you can do."

"Save her dear tree!"

"I can't. My power comes from love, only your love, it can't be turned into another. Love is oneness, which gives

56

me power when I am beside you. Your name is carved on my trunk. Love can't be lent or passed on to others like a property. Love's heart can only live in the beloved's chest. Love is one and there is no two. But the dark roots of Palid tree are fed by hatred, and hatred acts alone in isolation. It is like a fire in the forest, it burns everything. It is its nature, it can't avoid it."

"If that's so, I want Palid to take me instead of Apana. I'll trade myself for her."

"Nana, don't you remember the little Div? He is the child of Palid tree that is inside of Apana. Your sister's body is a temporary home for this immature fruit, and now it is time for Div's birth and his return to home. Palid will never leave her child. These black roots will return Dive to her mother, Palid tree, today, tomorrow or ten years later. These roots will suck on Apana's blood and make her so sick that she will sooner or later give it up. The little Div belongs to the darkness.

Nana snapped the last black root from her sister's body and threw them to where they had come from. Nana, injured and tired, was alert and breathing heavily. Padid tree treated Nana's wounds. The two lovers spent an hour filling Apana's room with the healing magic of love, like lighting a candle in the dark.

It was morning again; another opportunity to spend a new day with Apana.

CHAPTER 26

Crying is the Mirror of Laughter

The next morning, Apana looked very weak and tired. She had no words to speak. Both her hands had a variety of serums that were connected, a tube had been inserted into her nose for food, another tube was in front of her nose for oxygen, and a tube from the abdomen emptied the blood. Tests showed she had severe anemia, so the doctors prescribed a few more units of blood.

Nana was very worried and her eyes were the narrators of her suffering in her heart. Apana looked at Nana and complained: "Where is that strong, determined woman whom I met the first day here?"

Nana tried to dominate her feelings but it was too late. Her tears were dropping from her face. Apana cried too. She was crying for everything. For her life, the golden and current opportunity, like a river that would never return to its source and like the last grains of sand that were falling down from the upper part of an hourglass.

Nana took Apana's hands and kissed them kindly: "Excuse me, I didn't mean it. But sometimes it's not bad to cry. Crying is like a rain that washes all the dust of sorrow from your soul. After the rain, there are water ponds that mirror the sky in themselves and the tears reflect the beauty of your heart. The healing cry caresses your face with its wet fingers. My dearest, crying eyes are so beautiful when the story of the heart and soul is narrated and revealed. What a miserable and pitiful creature is one who is unable to cry!"

Apana agreed. She needed to cry too. Shortly afterwards both were lighter. Blood had been injected and Apana was now looking better. Their eyes glowed brighter after the salty rain.

The Most Beautiful

Nana and Apana had a strange feeling. They wanted to be indifferent about what might happen next. They were trapped like being on a small iceberg in a vast sea; floating and wandering, they had no choice but to wait. On one hand the sun was wonderful, but on the other hand it melted the ice beneath them. The piece was getting smaller and smaller, but the two sisters decided to live in the moment to appreciate the chance of being together. They hoped that enjoying each other's company and sharing sincere love would sustain them. This was how they spent their days.

But pain, the everlasting companion of mankind, was also constant. Apana experienced a kind of pain that is impossible to describe, and Nana felt another pain in her heart and soul that was like torture. Complaints were silenced because they knew the pain was not important. What mattered was how to deal with the pain. Pains always come and go for different reasons at different times, but what makes a person more special than others is his unique way of dealing with pain. Will they surrender or fight to the last moment? It is human nature to choose what to do. At these points, the most beautiful moments can be built when the human faces their pain.

So Apana asked Nana to tell her another story in order to enjoy the opening of another revelation, having a look inside it and forgetting the pain.

CHAPTER 28

The Deal

Nana began the story by saying: "Once upon a time there was a city where people were unaware of the beauty of dreams. There was a woman who could live in her dreams that were not possible in her real life. The world of dreams was mysterious and light. Real life was harsh and dark. One day, the woman found a man who loved dreams too. So they got married and after a while, the woman became pregnant and that brought her back to the real life, which was full of colors and light at that moment.

One day when the woman was alone in the house, the doorbell rang. The woman went to the door and asked: "Who is it?"

A violent voice from behind the door replied: "It's me, the great Div, I've come to get your baby."

The woman stepped back then put her hands on her belly and thought a little. She opened the door and stared at Div's eyes and said: "No, I'm not going to give my baby to you. Go away from here! You can't scare me!"

Dive said: "I am strong and you are a weak woman."

The woman said: "I am not afraid because I am a mother and mothers are the most powerful creatures in the world." Then she thought a little and said: "But now that you've come here, let's make a deal!"

"What deal? How can you and I make a deal? Divs don't deal, they just get what they want."

The woman said: "No, that's not true. If it was so, you wouldn't be here. The blackmail itself is a kind of deal. You wanted my child instead of your roughness and savagery. Isn't that true?"

Div scratched his head and thought. "That's right, blackmail can be a bargain. But I don't know another deal?"

The woman said: "There is no need to know because the existence of the world is based on taking and giving things instead. We trade childish innocence for the independence of youth. And we spend our youthful energy on prosperity in old age. The rest of death is preferable to the disability of aging. Sometimes it seems fair that we call it 'justice' and sometimes it doesn't seem fair, so it is called 'inequity.' Even convincing someone that you are being fair in a false deal is also a deal."

Divs were unlikely to hear or understand such things, but there was something in the woman that had transformed the Div. Without any desire he made a deal that he would be able to understand, feel and not be savage. So he told her: "Okay, whatever you want."

The woman said, "Don't take my baby and I'll immortalize you in return. I'll take you to the world of stories one day and you'll always be a part of me, my child and the whole world."

The great Div cried. Divs should never look into the eyes of a pregnant women because those eyes are professional alchemists. He was in pain, screaming, and turned to smoke, and he went up into the air. And no one ever saw the great Div who was no longer a Div.

Nana was looking out the window. A little farther out of the room, she saw the great Div watching her. It was a wandering Div who had been banished from the land of darkness as a curse forever. The great Div was the one who had talked to the little Div. He was not successful. Had a fair deal been done that night? Apana's life instead of the little Div's returning home? A teardrop slipped from Nana's eye and the great Div's eye. What could be the next deal?

CHAPTER 29

Silence is the Last Step

The mood of those days in their room was more silent. Apana sank deeper away and she talked less. Nana also made the narrator of her thousand and one night stories to be quiet.

Sometimes the greatness of the pain makes you remain silent.

Sometimes it was better to be silent and to say nothing. Sometimes silence speaks more than any words. Sometimes there is no explanation but silence.

And of course there are the silences that arise from the vanity of any meaning that cannot be expressed by any words.

How could Apana tell her everlasting beloved sister that she longed for her last goodbye? How could Nana dare to deceive her with lies about recovery? Her heart chose not to give up hope but there were some facts about Apana's condition that Nana was not facing honestly.

So in silence, Apana went into a coma.

CHAPTER 30

Cages

Sometimes your body is the cage of your soul. Sometimes the room you are in is the cage of your body. And sometimes the love that gives you life becomes your cage. There is a strange relationship between humans and cages. Nana thought keeping a yellow canary in a cold iron cage was a painful message about the eternal captivity of mankind in himself.

Was the spirit of Apana eager to fly from her cage or was she was used it? Did her soul have a desire to fly or was she afraid of leaving? Nana didn't know what to pray for at that moment: to be free from her suffering body or to stay in a broken and ruined cage.

Nothing was known except that the two sisters, like two captive birds, were trapped in a cage called room 215 at the Hotel of God.

CHAPTER 31

The Resurrection

The day of the resurrection of Christ, Apana's heart stopped and her last breath flew out of her chest like a little bird. A simple and innocent flight.

Nana screamed with all her might. She didn't know if Apana could hear her or not. It was as if the iceberg they had been on had broken in two and she was watching Apana sink. Nana begged Apana not to leave her alone in that cold and strange land, but the roots of Palid tree had taken Apana and the little Div who had grown in her belly back to an unknown place.

Doomsday means you hear the world's greatest symphonies, but you don't care. Mountains dance and seas fly in front of your eyes but you don't mind at all, because something much more important has happened. An event that leaves you half human. You have half heart, half spirit and even somehow half body.

Resurrection means all your possessions, your spirit, your experiences, your faith and your endurance have been changed. Your entire ideology and belief system has been turned upside down. It means that you are at the edge of darkness and light; you are at once a believer in God and a total atheist. Sometimes you are between them.... Resurrection means to awaken from a sweet and cheerful sleep and open your eyes to the world of the naked and nightmarish reality .... It's the return of man from the world of ignorance and simplicity to the world of bitter facts that you have just come to understand ... It was a very painful breakdown. And it was the beginning of an angelic resurrection whose wings were burned and she had fell down in the land of mortality.

CHAPTER 32

The Return

There was nothing left in the Hotel of God. In the remaining half of Nana, there was a motherly heart that was beating for Dara. She left the cage without her other half. She looked up to the dark sky. It was so cold, but a volcano was erupting inside. She had taken off the warm wolf skin that the native man had given her on her arrival, which had allowed her to conquer that cold snowy land. There was no snow, the rain had washed away all the snow.

She said: "It's too late!"

Then she howled like a wolf. No doubt the wolves were crying like that. Shortly afterwards the wolf with fiery eyes came to her without the native man. Nana hugged him and the wolf put his head on Nana's shoulder. By the morning the two wolves were heard roaring.

CHAPTER 33

Atlas

The next morning, Nana was like an angel with burned wings. An angel who drank from the spring of heavenly green lands and was flying delightfully until yesterday when she had opened her eyes to the cruel reality of her decent into the desert of suffering the next morning. The pleasure of flying was no more.

Nana was like a black hole that was created by the destruction of a star. A black hole that could drag everything into its darkness and destroy it.

Nana was like an invisible creature that the world could not see, but she dragged and killed the light of the universe in her darkness.

Nana was like the cursed Atlas of the gods who was condemned to keep the earth on his shoulders forever. Who had wished to turn into a stone but could be released from the curse.

CHAPTER 34

The Waterfall

Nana must have fallen asleep because she didn't notice when the wolf had gone. The native man who had met her when she arrived in the snowy land was coming towards her. Without any words he took Nana's hands. Through that contact Nana was able to see the man's ancestors while they were passing through a lighted tunnel. They were the true children of nature. Nana was surprised to feel something inside her heart. She felt the "mother of the earth."

Then the native man took her up to a huge waterfall. The greatness of the waterfall conquered Nana's soul. She was amused by that green, glassy water for a while, but she soon felt the pain in her heart again.

The man pointed to the snow that was melting and said: "The snow melts, falls from the height of the mountains and creates this wonderful beauty. Unless you fall into the deep valley, you will not be beautiful. This message is for you, this is your way."

Nana had to make a decision. She remembered the naked woman on the bridge who had jumped down. What was really that woman's pain?

The native man pointed to the waterfall: "The way back home!"

Nana looked a little at the huge, flowing and glassy waterfall then jumped into the mighty stream.

At the last moment she heard the native man say: "Always go on and on!"

CHAPTER 35

Thousands and Thousands of Drops

As soon as she hit that huge, glassy, green water, she felt that like a crystal piece on the waterfall rocks that was broken into thousands upon thousands of drops, followed by the explosive sound that was lost in the glittering and deafening roar of the waterfall. Nana felt as light as the tiny droplets of water scattered in space. She didn't know who she was, where she came from or where she would go. Nothingness was exactly what she needed. At that moment she was one with that absolute beauty, power and uniqueness. Waterfalls are the most magnificent, beautiful and ultimate bodies of water in the world. Waterfalls are the farewell to the ground and returning to the arm of it. Waterfalls are the flight of waters again after the fall of rain.

CHAPTER 36

The Unmasked Land

Down the waterfall where the river was a little calmer, the bare and half-dead Nana was lying on the rocky shore in the arms of Padid tree's roots. Her hair was dancing slowly in the water and Padid tree was caressing her with its healing branches. Hearing a sound coming from the trees nearby, Padid tree covered Nana's body with a green robe of its leaves and went back slowly to the river and disappeared.

Someone came up to Nana's head: "Get up Nana. Welcome to the unmasked land."

Nana opened her eyes and touched the soft green robe. She barely raised her head and looked at the strange but familiar woman who was facing her. Then with eyes wide open, she said: "The ladybird lady?"

The woman said: "Oh, you recognized me, well done!" Then she gave Nana a cup of coffee and said: "I know your memories of me are not so good. Sometimes I was unkind to you. Can you forgive me?"

Nana was silent for a while. The only sense of anger that she could still feel in her heart was about losing Apana. She couldn't do anything about it and about Palid tree who took her sister away. So she nodded and forgave the old woman.

The ladybird lady smiled and said: "As I said, this is the unmasked land, and it is clear why. You can see everyone as how they are on the inside, without any masks. For example, I can see your bright spirit that tries to be harmonious and kind with nature. Your heart is one of the rare hearts that cannot be found in your kind, I mean human beings. You are somehow a child of the Earth. So, dear Nana, be aware that you have lots of friends here. Drink your coffee and go along the river. Trust in the river! It will guide you in the proper time."

Then she looked at Nana with respect and turned away. The ladybird lady in her red and black dress disappeared in the darkness of the trees by the river. How had she realized Nana's suffering? Was it true that everything was visible in the unmasked land? If so, what were hearts and souls like with no mask?

Nana tasted her coffee. It was sweet and warm. She watched the river in silence.

CHAPTER 37

How the Rivers Die

Watching and listening to the river for a long time took Nana into a trance. Invisible strings of time and place were opened from her soul, and she could see the fate of the rain and snow after falling on the ground and melting and flowing down from the mountains as small springs and streams. Nana was able to see how large and wide rivers were formed out of these shallow and insignificant streams. The rivers, these veins of the Earth, were the hosts of huge lands, people and many creatures. Many bitter and sweet events happened during their journey. Nana saw many temples that were built beside the holy land of the rivers. Various religions and beliefs were connected to them. By bathing in the water, they hoped that their sins would be washed away. They also threw the ashes of their dead into their eternal home of the water. A little lower, perhaps, were farmers who donate gifts in the rivers to bless their lands and harvests. Or the fishermen whose lives depended on the generosity of them and the metropolises that for centuries had been born because of the blessing of the rivers. Whatever they were, nothing could prevent them of flowing. The dynamics were the inherent essence of the rivers. The low, continuous sound of the river became a beautiful song for Nana that said: "Let pass and go, forgive and let pass ... let go and pass, forgive and pass!" Nana's soul started to dance along the river until she reached the bottom of the river .... The river ended in the embrace of the sea. In the embrace of the indigo sea. So it was there. The rivers die in the embrace of the sea.

Nana came out of the trance. She was still sitting by that great river. Her heart was blackened by the rage and hatred of Palid tree.

The river was dynamic and flowing. It was lively and large. The dynamic and profitable lives of the rivers had made the rivers to deserve such a beautiful death, the river death.

CHAPTER 38

Prince Zaal

"**G**et up Nana and move on!" yelled a young man said who was rushing toward her. Nana stood up impatiently and noticed the roots of Palid tree that were so near her legs.

Surprised, Nana asked: "What do they want? I don't have any Div in my abdomen i, do I?"

The white haired man looked at her in amazement and said: "Div?"

The young man's surprised facere minded Nana of some one. Where could she have met him before? Nana answered: "It is a strange and long story. Have we met before?"

The man replied, "Maybe! That could be a strange story too."

Then the man pointing to the green robe of Padid tree on Nana continued: "Of course, with this robe, there will be no serious danger to you. It has been made of love."

The young man reached out to shake hands. Nana took his hand and suddenly felt a strange and familiar sensation. She knew him from somewhere but could not recognize where at that moment.

"I am Prince Zaal by the way!" he said. "In this land there are specific laws for everyone, and the law is 'to move' from here. I will accompany you the days and nights if you allow me."

Since long before the beginning of her journey Nana learned to welcome events and signs without questioning so she agreed to continue the rest of her journey with Prince Zaal.

*Zaal in Farsi is a person who is born with completely white hair. It is also the name of a mythical king.

CHAPTER 39

The Meditation

Prince Zaal had a very good characteristic of not being very talkative. Nana was comfortable with him and could behave however she wanted. Whenever she wished to whisper a song, Zaal continued to walk like a deaf creature beside her not disturbing her at all. He was just walking patiently beside her. The only time that Zaal broke his silence was when he wanted to remind Nana to keep moving — the law of the unmasked land for Nana. Nana sometimes nagged and refused when she was tired or hopeless but the kind and persistent insistence of Prince Zaal could convince her to start walking again.

The river and their uneventful walk led Nana to a deep meditation. Nana remembered the wild white geese who told her how on long flights in the silence of the sky, they could hear the voices of their hearts and the voices of other spirits.

Although Nana did not know the real reason for Prince Zaal's arrival in her life, she believed that it was essential despite the constant and unrestful pain of walking. He connected her to her lost inner self.

CHAPTER 40

The Invitation

In one of her meditations, Nana dreamed of a strange scene. A large, open mouth with a book inside it invited Nana to come inside and read the book. Near dusk, they reached a large cave that was visible through the dense foliage of trees. Nana noticed the resemblance between the cave and the mouth in her dream. She took a step toward the cave, glanced at the prince and asked: "Aren't you coming?"

Zaal replied: "This invitation is for you only. I'll wait here."

Nana thought a little. A strong temptation forced her to go into the cave, so she stepped inside. As soon as she entered, the roots of the Padidtree surrounded her and quickly dragged her deep into the cave.

CHAPTER 41

The Hands with Candles

Nana screamed with all her might, but something dragged her down the narrow, dark tunnel. She had the feeling that she was getting sucked by a black hole. Her hands grasped for hold in vain. She didn't know how long the journey into the dark depths of the Earth took, but after a while it ended. The roots left her and disappeared. When Nana's eyes were able to see in the darkness, she saw a wide empty field with no plants ended to two huge mountains leaning on each other. There was a stairway was just below the two mountains that led up to a cave. It was dark but not cold. She couldn't hear a sound and she felt surrounded by magic. It was like being at the Batu Caves but it was nighttime and there were no pilgrims. Dark. Magnificent. She felt weightless, as if she were dreaming.

A voice from behind her ordered gently: "Go up the stairs, there is someone waiting for you."

Nana turned around and saw the naked woman who had jumped off the bridge at beginning of Nana's journey. She looked calm and beautiful in a long gown.

Nana asked: "Who is waiting for me?"

The woman replied: "You will find out."

She accompanied Nana down the stairs. "Why did you throw yourself down that night," Nana asked.

The woman said: "There are some pains in the world that are greater than the human spirit, and sometimes a man achieves his liberation by destroying his body to free his soul. Freedom is a great motivation."

Nana didn't ask any more questions. She knew the pain that she was talking about could be overwhelming. Lack of love is the greatest pain of all.

The closer they got to the stairs, the more they plunged into the darkness. There in front of them, where they were going toward, were two rows of lighted candles on both side of the stairs. The rows of candles were continoued up to the top of the stairs. With the help of the enormous lighted candles that were placed on the palms of open hands on either side of the stairs, it was brighter. It was strange for Nana because she could just see the open palms of hands in two rows without being able to see the owner of the hands with the burning candles on them. After a long climb, they finally made it to the top. When they reached the final step, the woman said to Nana: "From here on, you have to go alone. I am not allowed to enter."

CHAPTER 42

The Light Tunnel

As Nana climbed another flight of stairs, the previous stairs disappeared. She couldn't turn around, but she could feel a warm trust in her heart. A voice asked her to take the robe off and get naked. Nana disrobed and continued walking. She felt light as she began to rise from the ground. She was immersed in the light. Then a force drove shot her into a tunnel of light like a meteorite through the sky. When finally came to a stop she was looking at a land of infinite beauty.

CHAPTER 43

The Children of 'Truth'

A moth that was purple and pink and had turquoise blue spots greeted Nana.

Nana smiled at him and asked: "Do I know you?"

"You haven't seen me, but you know me," the moth replied. "But it's better not to ask for more. There is sometimes some comfort in not knowing some things."

In front of them, between the ground and the sky, there was something like a large tree. Beautiful waterfalls flowed from up to down like its roots, each of them divided into several cascades. Instead of leaves there were thin strings that became gradually invisible as they got farther from the semi-tree creature.

"What are those strings?" Nana asked.

"Oh, you know them, the 'invisible strings.' That is 'Truth,'" he said pointing to that huge semi-tree.

Nana looked at the waterfalls. There was a bright, pleasant fog more or less. Although there was no sun or any light source there was a celebration of blue, green and purple light. It was so vast and incredible that Nana gasped. For a moment she even forgot about Apana and the reason for her being there. She saw many people in different groups at the bottom of each cascade. A band was involved in a kind of dance ceremony. The other group was sitting and whispering words in a monotonous voice. One group was watching the waterfall with love and sorrow. There was also a group of singers and a group of prayers. A group with books and tools were doing something similar to research and discussion. Near one of the cascades a group were naked and making love.

Nana asked the moth: "Who are these people and what are they doing?"

They are the children of truth. Each group is worshiping according to their understanding of the truth. Although all waterfalls originate from the truth, their interpretations, beliefs and practices are very different. They can only see part of the truth. What they see is right but incomplete. And of course, it's impossible to see the whole truth from down there.

Here in the unmasked world, although everything seems cluttered at first glance, it's like a big orchestra — they play amazing music because everyone in the world is an instrument in this symphony.

Watching Truth was fun and enjoyable. Within these heterogeneous groups, there was an overall order and coordination. As time went on, Nana noticed that Truth was turning very slowly, almost imperceptibly. It was like changing from day to night; subtle but constant. Little by little, Truth was rotating and revealing its other side. It was black and the waterfalls were like tar and the invisible strings were cut. At the foot of the waterfalls, a band of demons and Divs worshiped in their own way. Their voices, like bass notes, complemented the symphony of Truth. She turned toward the moth to ask what was going on, but she was surprised to see a small Div standing next to her. Nana remembered the roots of Palid tree. Her surprise instantly changed to anger. She remembered her great hatred of Palid tree and the little Div.

She shouted: "You? I have to kill you to let your mother feel how much I've suffered from the loss of my sister."

Little Div looked at her then he opened his chest and took out a glassy bubble and showed it to Nana. "Inside this glass is my life," he said. "I give it to you and you can break it and I'll die, but you can't get Apana back because she's not here."

Touching the glass of Div's life, Nana hesitated to break it. The opportunity for revenge had now come, but she couldn't kill Div. She had experienced many years ago that the true pleasure of revenge is in forgiveness.

Div said: "Days and nights are complementary. A painter, to emphasize the bright and luminous parts of his work, must use dark colors in the vicinity of the bright spot, otherwise how could you see the light? Can one understand 'good' while denying the existence of 'bad'? Without feeling hunger, how can one described satiety? The dualism of Truth is a must. These cannot be justifications for the cruelty of Palid tree."

Nana asked: "Why did you take my dear Apana?"

"I'm the son of Truth, which means I am also someone's child and dear to a mother. Whatever you know about Palid tree or Truth is one of the thousands of hallucinatory names that people chose for it. People want to discover the unlimited world through a small window. Your suffering made you unable to look fairly to the justice that exists in the world. How sure are you that you see the whole story and your judgement is right? Sometimes people act just like the ignorant judge who judges without parties and without proper understanding of the case. They sentence an innocent person to death, which is injustice itself."

Nana did not said anything. She just cried.

CHAPTER 44

Hallucinatory Names

Div cleared Nana's tears with his thick and rough finger and continued: "My dear Nana, you will never reach your destination as long as you are stuck in your pain and sitting on the judge's seat. People have called Truth Palid, death, annihilation, injustice but understand that these titles only portray parts of the huge creature that is now in front of you. Is not death another face of life? A newly born baby gets closer to which one, life or death? Is the first breath the beginning of life or the calendar of death? Can this birth originate from nothingness to the world of beings? When something doesn't exist, how can it be a creature in the world itself?

"Dear Nana, we have always been and are and will be. We have not come from nothingness to existence. We are just transformed from one form to another. By Truth, I'm a moth, but on this side, I'm a Div. Dear Nana, we are plagued by names that are unfair prejudices. Truth is a whole and it is impossible to look at the details and get the perfect picture. It's useless to look for Apana in the known world. You won't find her here."

CHAPTER 45

A Kiss on Div's Forehead

Faced with the different faces of death and the simplicity of Div's nature, Nana plunged deep into thought. She remembered the punches she had thrown with anger into the air. She began to cry trying to understand the reasons for what had happened to her and the pain she still felt in her heart for her misery, her anger, her pain and loneliness, and her unanswered questions.

Truth was gradually turning around, and the little Div was standing beside her patiently and without saying a word. Nana slowly calmed down and looked at the big change that was happening in front of her face.

"Sufferers and the unknown can change over time. Sufferings can change and change is the identity of life and immortality. Death is a change and means transition from stationary, so death is also a process of immortality. Sufferers are dear, deaths can be sweet."

Nana asked: "How can death be sweet or immortality? Death means I don't see her and that means she's no longer with me. No matter where she is, I can't see her anymore. And it's painful."

Div smiled, which softened his rough face a little bit. "What is causing you pain is getting caught in the past or in the future. Don't be a prisoner of time, the past or the future. Take the chance of being alive and challenge your life for today. This is your way and your life. Don't sell it for free. Your questions will remain a mystery forever. No human will find a right answer for death and the aftermath.

"And about suffering; a good gardener sometimes prunes his flowers. They prune the branches, or even transplant it from place to place. New trees come from this pruning. Extracting their roots and planting them in new soil in another corner of the garden cause the plant to fade for a while, but in the end a beautiful garden with fertile trees is the result of this suffering. One cannot deny the benefits of suffering. Sometimes suffering is a challenge to move and change. I see beautiful light in your eyes and of course a few lines below, which can be the result of aging or too much crying. These lines are beautiful too."

And with his fingers he erased the last tears from Nana's face.

Nana looked at the little Div and kissed his forehead. She bowed to the marvelous Truth and said goodbye. When she lifted her head, she found herself in front of the cave where Prince Zal was waiting for her.

CHAPTER 46

Trust

Prince Zal was very happy to see Nana. He hugged Nana warmly. Nana was happy too, but she was still confused about what she had experienced in the cave. Some of her questions were answered but not from the point of view she used to have. They were answered from a distance observer's perspective. She also understood that some of her questions would never be answered. Most importantly, she knew she was not alone; she shared many of her questions, her suffering and her experiences with other people. Many in the world looked the same. Nana now realized she had never been left alone on that path. There was a great wisdom behind all her adventures, as well as the many invisible strings in her life.

A sweet change that felt like trust swept over Nana. She trusted that she was never left alone. She no longer considered herself lost in the unknown world alone.

The house must be close by, she thought. She longed for it.

Zal said: "Let's go, dear friend." He smiled, and they found the path along along the river again.

CHAPTER 47

Happiness is the Reward of Fulfilling Your Duty

The banks of the river was steep and the water ran fast. A group of fish were slowly making their way in the opposite direction of the river. Nana stood watching them. A fish was trapped in a shallow tide pool near Nana. It appeared she was breathing her last breath but it wouldn't take much effort to save herself.

Nana asked: "Do you need help?"

She replied: "No, this is the end of our journey to reproduction, and our task in nature is over."

Nana asked in surprise: "How? It looks like suicide; don't you have another way to reproduce?"

Fish said: "Sometimes in life you should not ask. Where do you come from and where will you go? My duty is birth, life and continuity of the next generation. The seed doesn't care if it is in a pot or a grove. It just grows happily for its predetermined mission. Happiness is to do the duties you were sent her for. I will continue in my next generation, so I accept it and do it happily."

Nana looked more closely at the group of the fish that were jumping across the river from that steep slope. Their cheerful effort was like a dance along the river. An hour later, the fish had completed their mission.

CHAPTER 48

The Story of Zaal

It might have been thirty-nine days that Zaal and Nana were walking along the river. Nana could smell the sea. Her pain had gradually diminished in the constant strolls and unwanted meditations of this long and steady journey along the river. Nana had accepted her pains as a part of the unknown sides of her life, and she had learned to respect and trust in the law of life rather than fear or denial the unknown.

At one of the meditations, Nana saw her little dog, Charlie, that was begging for his daily walk in his special, sweet way. Nana came out of that revery and looked at Zaal. Charlie? His white hair, curly and all the walking? In his silence and loyalty, in the unmasked world Charlie was the Prince Zaal.

Nana looked at him and asked: "What's your story?"

Zaal smiled and said, "Then it's my turn. Before being a dog, I was a proud, selfish and vindictive prince. I broke too many hearts. But life gave me a chance to change. I died in an accident, and in my new life I became a dog, as you know. I got an owner whom I loved a lot, and I tried to be cute to get more attention from her. It was sometimes hard to obey her, to bear her rules that were against my nature, but I had no choice. She was sometimes a kind old woman to me, of course. Then she was swallowed by the darkness over the bridge, and it was a good opportunity for me to get rid of the doggy life I had. But I saw you, lonely and frightened. It was not so difficult because you needed me. I decided to be your dog then and I didn't follow my old lady into the darkness."

Nana's eyes were full of tears. She did not know what to say so she simply responded: "You are the most loyal companion that I had on my journey."

Zaal's eyes glowed because of her sweet compliment. "Well, we have reached the sea but I can't leave the unmasked world in this shape and body that I have now. So goodbye to you. Take care! You will visit me again very soon."

Then he turned and disappeared behind the trees.

CHAPTER 49

The Displaced Div of the Tales

The sea, that huge, wild and calm blue water, was now in front of Nana. The waves were coming and going, kissing her feet. They were ecstatic and charming. The great Div who had been rejected by Palid tree for his choice to deal with Nana was there.

Nana walked over to him and said: "Forgive me, I didn't know that I made you become a wanderer in here and the other world with the choice I gave you."

Div answered: "Don't be regretful! Rebellion is beautiful, especially because of love."

The strange confession of Div's love shook Nana: "Who's love?"

Div said: "Never look into the eyes of a woman who has a child in her womb! Remember that?"

Nana said sadly: "I'm sorry."

"Don't be!" Div said. "The world of love is such a beautiful world that is not comparable to the two worlds you know. I am no longer a Div because of love. Out of this body, I am a dynamic energy and free from anyone else. Because of you, my existence shines in an eternal light. My dear Nana, you were a window into my world of love and rebelliousness. My life has received a color more beautiful than any other colors and a taste sweeter than all sweetness. I wasn't beautiful without you and now I am. And now I'm like this wide sea."

Div's words touched Nana's heart. Div was not the creature she had first met. He was not just a Div, it was a world of beauty.

After a little contemplation, Nana said to Div: "Promise me something!"

"What?"

Nana said: "Be the Div who takes me away someday. Of course, you are my choice to fly from this world to another."

"No, it's my turn to ask you something!" said Div.

Nana said: "Say it!"

Div gave Nana the glassy bubble of his life and said: "Please be the one as a human that will free me from being a Div."

It was difficult for Nana to accept it because she knew it would kill Div. She had learnt this from the stories her mother used to tell her years ago when she was a child.* She finally understood. It was her turn to listen to his request. So she took the glass of his life and

---

* In Persian myths the glassy heart of Divs are out of their body and if some one finds it and breaks it, he will die.

smashed it on the ground. The glass of life broke into a thousand pieces and each piece turned into blue drops of water and joined the sea. Div turned into white smoke and joined the white clouds above to rain over different lands as a blessing.

CHAPTER 50

The Ring

The sea looked at Nana with her wet eyes and asked: "What do you want?"

Nana said: "Crossing!"

The sea said, "I'll tell you the passage because I owe you. One day my waves snatched from a ring from your slim fingers that your mother had given to you. Do you remember?"

Nana remembered that bitter old memory. Once she had a journey with her family to a seaside in her motherland. There she lost her ring when she was swimming. After that, whenever she met any body of water she would complain in her heart about the waves because of her lost ring. For Nana, all the seas were the same and connected. There at the end of the unmasked land that sea knew her old story and tried to help.

But nothing is lost anywhere in the world. The old sea made up the lost ring giving a hint of password. Yesterday's little Nana had lost so many things more important than that ring that the memory of her lost ring was not hurting her anymore. She wished all the things that she had lost were as insignificant as that ring.

But nothing seemed to be lost anywhere in the world, not a little girl's ring or her abandoned land and even the wings her man left behind the iron gate. She had learned through her life that there are no mistakes, no lost in the world. So she was not surprised about what the sea told her.

CHAPTER 51

Dance of Fire on The Water

The sea told Nana: "The way to pass me is the dance of fire."

Nana kept silent, as she had learned from the goose. Silence was the key to hearing the answer that she knew was beside every question. She sat down on the sandy beach and stared into the sea. The sun shone on the raging surface of the sea where the flames were dancing. She found the answer and immediately jumped into the water and let herself float on the sea. Like waves on the water, she let herself be free without any effort and was accompanied by the flames that turned out to be the reflected sunshine on the water. She looked at the sky and filled with the light, the dance, and the blue of the sky. With the dance of the waves, she also danced and shone. Letting the sea guide her, Nana was slowly drifted away from the shore.

CHAPTER 52

Devotion

The sea was always a huge horror for Nana. The huge blue water with all the creatures inside it was always the most frightening for her. The sea and the sky above it were nothing but great blues. It was as if she was enclosed in a very large, blue bubble. She felt small, and she wept that she was nothing in that world, even a dot in the universe. Day gradually became night. The sky at night seemed even bigger. Nana knew that some stars had been extinguished long years before their light reached Earth, but she could still see them. They were so far but remained a point in the sky. Nana knew there were other galaxies besides that galaxy — millions of them. The galaxies were so big the great stars were even a spot in front of them.

The fear in the night grew larger and Nana felt smaller and smaller. Nana looked at her own little world. Apana's grief was not that significant against these huge giants. Everything was in vain for her. All the greed, pleasure, stress and war. All of them were so small and unimportant for her in front of these great, great things. Nana was immersed in nothingness and also in the seawater until the next morning. She had surrendered herself to the sea and her fate. It carried her to a place where no one knew.

Plankton

Huge pods of whales approached Nana. These beautiful and majestic animals were much larger than they had been in the photos and movies Nana had seen. Their kind eyes were as gray as two large marbles. Their mouths were as big as a cave. Nana was afraid of being swallowed by the whales or drowned by the wake from the huge tails of the whales. But they were skillful swimmers.

One of them said: "Don't be afraid, Nana! Our little friend! We just eat plankton."

Nana knew that. Suddenly she remembered her feeling of smallness the previous night. Plankton, the tiny particles in the great ocean, were the most important part of the food chain in the nature, especially for these big creatures.

The whales said: "Small or big, they are all chained together. No one is more important in this chain. Everyone has a different role. Nothing in the world is insignificant. The fly or a butterfly can be the cause of a storm somewhere on the Earth. A simple smile can make a difference in the world. All of us have been chained together, and a smile will make thousands of other people's days better. A song may make rain somewhere. We all are the creators and architects of this world. Make the world beautiful with your words. Dance when you sing. No matter who sees or knows, the important thing is that nothing will be lost. Happiness brings happiness and sadness brings sadness. We come to this world to add beauty. So beautiful dear Nana!"

Those words touched Nana's heart. Undoubtedly there was a reason of her coming to the world although she did not know what it was. And undoubtedly she was supposed to play an important role in the world, no matter how small or insignificant.

She watched the whales eat happily and enthusiastically. The contrast of beauty was there in the interaction of the biggest and smallest creatures of the sea, the plankton and the whales.

CHAPTER 54

A Land Called the World

The next morning, the waves had changed and her body could feel the sand. She sat up. She had reached the shore. She heard a dog's voice and the cheerful shout of a child too. It was the sound of her little son. Her little family were coming to welcome her happily. Nana was a little surprised. So where's the bridge? The foggy land? It was a sunny day. A little farther from Dara and Charlie, she saw her man coming toward her with a young woman. Nana tried to look more closely, but Charlie and Dara reached for her and hugged her warmly. Charlie wagged his tail and barked happily.

Dara gave the flower in his hand to his mother and said slowly in her arms: "Mom, I thought you wouldn't come back anymore!"

Nana tucked his brown hair behind his ears. He still smelled like a child. Infinite and silky. Slowly she said: "I'll never leave you alone, my life!"

Then she looked at her man and the woman he was with, who were getting closer at the time. That woman was Apana. She was wearing a long, pink dress and a flower ring in her loose hair.

Apana happily embraced Nana and said: "Welcome, Nana."

Nana was confused. How could that be?

Apana noticed her sister's wonder so she said: "My invisible strings of time and place have been cut. I can go everywhere, but I like to stay with you here in your house. I will stay with you as long as you are here."

Tears streamed from Nana's eyes. Then her husband greeted her and continued, "Let's go home! It's as clean and tidy as you always keep it. It is time to celebrate!"

They walked toward the house. It looked warmer and younger, with cherry and apple trees blossoming. Nana just looked out of her kitchen window where she used to watch the bridge. There was no bridge. For a while, she wondered where the bridge could have gone. Then she thought of the things that she used to think existed but in fact they didn't. She remembered those unsolvable problems, fears, beliefs and the borderlines and nationalities. She thought of so many things she had lost somewhere in her life, like the snowflake melting on her hand at the beginning of the bridge. There was never any bridge. Nana knew that there were so many made-up names in the world. Names like race, nationality and borders. There was no land that needed a bridge to connect to it. There was only one land, a land called the world.

The end.

www.ingramcontent.com/pod-product-compliance
Lightning Source LLC
Chambersburg PA
CBHW050955050726
47592CB00007B/2586